With special thanks to Allan Frewin Jones

For Brendan, for all his help

ORCHARD BOOKS

First published in Great Britain in 2019 by The Watts Publishing Group

1 3 5 7 9 10 8 6 4 2

Text © 2019 Beast Quest Limited
Cover illustrations by KJA Artists © Beast Quest Limited 2019
Inside illustrations by Dynamo © Beast Quest Limited 2019

Beast Quest is a registered trademark of Beast Quest Limited
Series created by Beast Quest Limited, London

A CIP catalogue record for this book is available from the British Library.

ISBN 978 1 40835 787 3

Printed in Great Britain

The paper and board used in this book are made from wood from responsible sources

Orchard Books
An imprint of Hachette Children's Group
Part of The Watts Publishing Group Limited
Carmelite House, 50 Victoria Embankment, London EC4Y 0DZ

An Hachette UK Company
www.hachette.co.uk
www.hachettechildrens.co.uk

THE

DARK WIZARD

ORCHARD

MEET THE GUARDIANS

SAM

BEAST POWER: Fire
LIKES: The beach
DISLIKES: Being told what to do

AMY

BEAST POWER: Storm
LIKES: Sports
DISLIKES: Injustice

CHARLIE

BEAST POWER: *Water*
LIKES: *Puzzles*
DISLIKES: *Heights*

PROLOGUE

The clattering rotor blades churned the air as the helicopter rose into the night sky over London. The black finger of Obsidian Tower rapidly fell away, the bright pinpoints of its helipad merging into the vast dazzle of the sleepless city lights.

Illia Raven turned her eyes away from Grom, the bulky stone pilot, and glowered at her boss. Malvel was smiling down at an amulet resting in his palm. It was made of brown metal, with a fine silver chain. A red jewel throbbed at its heart, throwing ruby light on to his face.

The Dark Wizard – known on Earth as Alistair Haynecroft, CEO of the powerful global company Obsidian Corp – seemed pleased, though Illia couldn't understand why.

She leaned forward, her red fringe falling over her eyes. "May I speak?" she asked, her anger bubbling.

Malvel didn't look up. "If you must," he replied.

"Why wasn't I allowed to join the fight against the Guardians?" Illia burst out.

"I'm not without power!"

Malvel looked at her and she shivered. There was a purple glow in his eyes which she had never seen before. "You call those scraps of magic that I have given you, *power*?"

Illia Raven was head of Obsidian's Research and Development Department, and with the "scraps of magic" the wizard had gifted her, she had created some very advanced tools and weapons.

"I could have helped," Illia replied. "Those three ... *children* ... fought back so hard that you had to escape from the roof!"

There was a deadly look in Malvel's eyes. "You think they defeated me?" He opened his palm and a ribbon of eerie green light spun across the cabin from his hand and wrapped around Illia's throat.

She clawed at it, gasping for breath.

"That is a taste of the power I drew from the Shadow Panther Varla, Karita's Beast," Malvel said. He flicked his fingers and the choking coil evaporated. He held up the amulet. "And this is the Seeing Eye. I tore it from the neck of one of the Guardian children."

"What does it do?" gaped Illia, rubbing her throat.

Malvel muttered a few words, causing the red jewel to send out flickering magical images around the helicopter's cabin.

There were landscapes, buildings, people's faces – Illia gasped as she caught sight of rows of skulls, and a coiled serpent. "It reveals to me the location of every Beast egg on this planet," Malvel replied. "I was not *driven* from my Tower, I took what I needed and left Karita and her pathetic Guardians to weep over their losses." His eyes gleamed. "Now we will roam the world at will, hunting down the Beast eggs one by one, until I have them all in my grasp."

"And then ... ?" Illia breathed. "Will you capture one of the child Guardians and have them hatch the eggs for you?" Malvel had told her that only Guardians had the ability to hatch Avantian Beast eggs.

Malvel was silent for a few moments. "I took the power of the Shadow Panther," he said at last. "It flows through my veins." Illia bit her lip as she saw the sinister purple light burn more fiercely in the Dark Wizard's eyes. "I might now be able to hatch the eggs myself," the wizard continued, "absorbing their power, becoming stronger and stronger!"

"And when you have all that power," said Illia, "will you return to Avantia?"

Illia was human, but she knew that portals could be opened between realms, and she knew that Malvel's ultimate intention was to return to his home world and become the Tyrant of Avantia.

When the Earth is mine and its people kneel before me, I will go back and fulfil my destiny!"

"When you leave Earth, you will need a trusted lieutenant to rule in your place," Illia said.

Malvel looked narrowly at her. "Would you like that to be you?"

"I would!" Illia exclaimed. "I will rule this planet in your name, and anyone who defies me will be crushed."

A faint smile curled Malvel's lip. "Grand words, Illia," he said. "But I will need proof that you are worthy."

Illia stiffened, her eyes blazing. "Try me!"

"Very well," said the Wizard. "I will give

you a mission to test your abilities – and to get those Guardian children out of the way ... *for ever.*"

Illia Raven leaned forward eagerly. If the three children had to die to prove her worth, then Amy Errinel-Li, Charlie Colton and Sam Stonewin were doomed.

ONE

Amy opened the box where she kept her coils and processors at night. Taking them out, she fitted the processors behind her ears and placed the coils against her skull, feeling the usual slight pressure as the internal and external magnets of her cochlear implants locked.

Lastly, she drew a scarlet headband over her hair. The band stopped her processors from being knocked loose during strenuous exercise – and judging by the use of capitals in the text Charlie had just sent, hard physical activity wasn't out of the question. She looked again at her phone, reading the message.

I KNOW WHERE WE CAN FIND ANOTHER EGG. WE HAVE TO GO TO BRIGHTON. TRAIN FROM VICTORIA STATION AT 9 THIS MORNING. BRING YOUR BIKE. I'VE SPOKEN TO THE OTHERS.

Amy's heart thumped. She still couldn't believe it was all real – Beasts, magic and wizards. She recalled the dreadful battle in Obsidian Tower the previous night. The green light flashing from Malvel's fingers, the inhuman power of his stone bodyguards. The little dragon, Spark, zipping around, breathing flame. Her, Sam and Charlie fighting with the weapons that had transformed from their Arcane Bands. Karita's mighty shadow panther, Varla, roaring.

She was about to text back asking what she was supposed to tell her parents, when there was a knock at the bedroom door.

"Amy, are you in there? You need to get ready." Her mum peeped round the door. "Sam just called. He says you're late for your wildlife club field trip."

Wildlife club? Amy had no idea what her mum was talking about.

"Sweetie, you didn't even tell me about a field trip. Or a wildlife club, for that matter. But I'm glad you and Charlie are making Sam welcome. I know it wasn't easy for him, moving all the way from Los Angeles. He says there have been some rare sightings in Brighton recently? He sounded excited."

"Oh!" Amy understood. "Yes, um, Sam just can't get enough of that wildlife." Thinking of her cousin's love of his baby dragon, Amy was pleased to realise this was completely true.

"Anyway, you're late, so one of the other kids' mum is picking you up. She had a funny name. Karina, was it?"

Amy grinned. "Karita, Mum. Right, that's,

um, *Tom*'s mum." Tom, as in Avantia's famed Master of the Beasts, was the first name that popped into Amy's head. "I completely forgot about the trip. I'll get my things."

Amy texted Charlie back: ON MY WAY!

When her mum had left, Amy opened up her backpack, peering in wonder at the beautiful Beast egg that lay inside. It had remained nestled in a scarf since she'd rescued it from Obsidian Tower. The shell shimmered with rainbows of colours, as if made from stained glass, and Amy was worried it might be fragile. She bent her ear down, listening for a clue as to what lay inside. *Are you in there, little Beast?*

As a Guardian of the Errinel line, Amy was bonded to all Storm Beasts. *What are you?* There was no reply, no hint of any noise coming from the egg. She sighed. Downstairs, she heard the doorbell go, and after a few moments she could hear a woman's voice. *It's Karita!* Zipping the bag, she ran down the stairs.

"See you later," she said to her mum as she followed Karita out the door.

"And we must have Tom over some time." said Amy's mum to Karita as Amy fetched her bike.

The tall woman fiddled with her dark, purple-streaked hair, looking uncomfortable. "Er, of course, some time.

Tom would love to. I'll ask him when we get back to the car. I'm parked just around the corner."

"Have a nice day, sweetheart," her mother said to Amy. "Look after yourself – and don't get into any trouble!"

"I will, and I won't!" Amy replied, hoping the opposite wouldn't turn out to be true.

"Are you sure you know where the egg is?" Amy asked Charlie, who was sitting opposite her on the cluster of six train seats. Karita and Sam sat beside them.

Charlie looked round, checking again that they had the carriage to themselves.

"I'm sure."

"Malvel is out there searching as we speak," said Karita, stroking Varla, who lay on her lap. "We have to be certain we are not wasting time." Amy knew that Karita's strength was linked to the shadow panther, so when Malvel had stolen the Beast's magic, Karita had also been sapped of much of her strength. The poor Beast was now only the size of a domestic cat, its fur faded from dark blue to grey. Karita herself looked worn out.

Charlie held up his smartphone. "These are from the video I took when Malvel activated the Seeing Eye amulet at Obsidian Tower." He swiped through photos of the shimmering images that had been projected magically from the ruby. Amy let out a sigh of wonder as she saw a woman's golden face, a row of columns in a desert, and then a coiled sea serpent. *Clues to the location of every Beast egg in the world!*

"Check out the sea serpent," Charlie told them. "And now compare it to this." He took out a browned piece of paper from his bag. It was some kind of old poster. It had bold red writing: *Professor Colton's Mysterious Voyage. Experience the underwater maze of an illusionist. Featuring magic and myth! Only at Brighton Pier!*

An illustration of a large blue serpent

covered with green spines was in the middle of the poster. It looked exactly like the serpent shown by the amulet. Its mouth gaped wide, baring two long fangs.

"Wow!" exclaimed Sam. "Look at that, Spark!" The small dragon poked its black scaly head out from his backpack.

"This is no coincidence," said Karita.

Amy stared in amazement. "Charlie – where did you find that?"

"It was in the attic at home," Charlie explained. "I thought the sea serpent looked familiar, so I hunted around for it last night. Years ago, my grandad was an illusionist, sort of like a magician and tinkerer. He built all kinds of crazy inventions."

Amy grinned. "Maybe he kept an egg in his house, like my grandma did."

Charlie nodded. "His cottage is only a short bike ride from the railway station." Sadness clouded his face. "He died when I was six, but I remember the place really well – it was full of his inventions. The house was never sold ... Dad couldn't bear it."

"Once we're close, the egg will call to you," said Karita. "The same way Sam's egg called to him."

Charlie's eyes lit up. "Yes! I'll get to bond with my own Beast!"

Amy pressed her hands over the shape of the egg in her backpack. "Uh, Karita," said Amy. "I know you think the egg from

Obsidian Tower is mine – but I haven't heard a peep out of it."

"You know there are many ways to communicate. It could be that because of your deafness, your Beast will speak to you differently," Karita suggested. "Have you tried touching it?"

Amy shook her head. "It looks so fragile."

Karita smiled. "Do not fear. It is stronger than you think."

Amy put the backpack on her lap and reached inside. The multi-coloured shell was warm against her fingers.

A soft whisper came into her mind, friendly and full of amusement.

Not just yet, it seemed to say. *But soon.*

"Oh!" Amy stared at her friends.

"Can you hear it? What's it sound like?" Charlie asked.

"It's more like a feeling. Like I already *know* it." Shivering with delight, Amy put her mouth to the open top of the backpack. "I'm right here," she whispered. "Don't worry, I'll look after you."

"Uh, guys," said Sam, staring out of the window. "What's *that*?"

Amy followed the line of his eyes.

Wha-a-at?

She stared in disbelief at the sight of two figures hanging beneath an X-shaped drone as it raced down from the sky towards the train.

One was the huge and horribly familiar figure of Grom, Malvel's stone bodyguard. The other was a slender woman, dressed in tight-fitting green leather and with spiky red hair tossed by the wind.

The drone hurtled towards the window of their carriage.

"Watch out!" shouted Amy.

Sam threw himself sideways, snatching at Spark. Charlie let out a yell. Cradling Varla, Karita hurled herself to the floor.

Amy just had time to fling her arms across her face as the window exploded inwards and a shockwave tossed her across the empty carriage.

The roar of the drone's engines almost

split her head. Splintered glass rained down. Gasping with shock, she saw the red-headed woman and her monstrous companion come down feet-first in the carriage.

The woman tapped a wristband and the drone detached itself and swept back out of the window. Grom loomed behind her.

The woman smiled down at them, her lips as red as blood in her white face. "My name is Illia Raven." She gestured to Grom. "This gentleman is already known to you, I think. Malvel has sent us here to kill you. Who's first?"

TWO

The sudden violence of the attack had left Sam dazed. His first thought had been to protect Spark, but the little dragon had moved just as quickly to defend *him*. She'd slipped from his backpack and swooped towards the red-haired woman, shooting a jet of flame from her mouth.

"Aww, the baby Beast," Illia Raven crooned, as she darted aside. "She is so *cute*." She raised her arm, aiming a small dark weapon the size of a TV remote control. A pulse of white light struck Spark, sending her spiralling down behind some seats.

A stab of anguish pierced Sam's heart. "No!"

He leaped up, flinging his arm towards the woman. His Arcane Band activated, and the metal hook spun out on its chain. He threw it towards Illia. As the hook whipped past her shoulder, Sam flicked his wrist and the chain wrapped around her neck.

She let out a cry of surprise and anger as she was almost wrenched off her feet.

"That's just rude!" she shouted, firing her weapon again.

Sam ducked as the white pulse sliced through the air above his head.

Illia raised her left hand. "Energy lance!" As though activated by her voice, a metre-long rod of green metal grew from her gloved fist. It was pointed at both ends, hissing and sparking with electricity.

Uh-oh!

She brought it down hard on Sam's chain. But the lance bounced off and she snarled in frustration.

Whatever that thing is – it doesn't work on Arcane Band weapons! Phew!

Grom hammered at him with a colossal fist. Sam dived aside. As the creature's great, flat inhuman face turned towards him, his eye-pits glowed green behind his dark glasses.

Sam knew what was coming – but he didn't have time to get out of the way.

The green light exploded from Grom's eyes, but in the split second before Sam was hit, Charlie sprang between them and the deadly fire beams glanced off the silver shield formed by his Arcane Band.

Although Sam's Fire bloodline made him immune to flame, that blast still would have thrown him the length of the carriage.

I could have been smashed to a pulp.

"Thanks!" Sam gasped.

"Don't mention – *oof!*" Charlie toppled

forwards as a flash of white light struck him from behind. He crashed to the floor unconscious, his shield dissolving back into his wristband.

While Sam had been distracted by Grom's attack, Illia had unwound the chain from around her neck and activated her weapon.

But before she could use it again, Amy and Karita charged at her. Amy had her mace in her hand, the spiked head slicing through the air as Illia backed off. Karita spun her bo-staff, whipping Illia's feet out from under her. But there wasn't enough room in the carriage for Karita to wield the staff decisively and Illia was soon up again, jabbing the energy lance into Karita's face, forcing her back along the aisle.

Illia brought the lance down hard. Karita jerked her head aside and the lance sliced through a seat.

Amy advanced fearlessly on Illia, whirling her mace as the red-haired woman warded off her blows with the energy lance.

"You fight well for a child!" Illia mocked.

"And you fight badly for a grown woman!" countered Amy, driving Illia back. Karita swung her staff and the pulse weapon was knocked from Illia's hand.

They're doing fine, and I have to get to Spark! Sam was afraid that his Beast might be badly hurt.

But before he could move, great stone arms encircled his chest from behind and he was lifted off his feet. He struggled, his arms pinned to his sides. Grom tightened his grip so that Sam could hardly breathe. He kicked wildly, fighting with every ounce of his strength. The pain was excruciating. Black stars exploded in front of his eyes.

A small shape darted over the seats, shrieking in anger.

"Spark!" gasped Sam. "You're OK!" The dragon had only been stunned. A dart of flame spurted from Spark's jaws, spraying into Grom's face.

Squirming in the stone man's grip, Sam wrenched himself to one side so that he

could jam his feet against the side of the carriage. Using his legs like pistons, he drove backwards.

Grom crashed down, Sam on top of him. Green fire shot from Grom's eyes, bursting through the carriage roof. But the stone man's grip loosened for a moment and Sam was able to rip himself free.

He remembered how they had dispatched Grom's twin in Obsidian Tower.

I need a shield to bounce his energy back at him!

At this thought, the hook and chain sank back into the Arcane Band and a round shield formed in its place. Using all his strength, Sam smashed the shield down on to Grom's face, hoping that the green fire would be mirrored into the stone man's eyes and destroy him.

But Sam wasn't strong enough to control the fires. The full force of Grom's blast threw him up through the broken carriage roof and out into the rushing air. Trees and telegraph poles flashed past as the train hurtled through the countryside.

With a yelp of alarm, Sam swapped the shield for a hook and chain. He managed to stab the hook into the roof before he was torn away by the train's speed. He came down hard, but was anchored firmly by the chain.

He glanced ahead. The train was shooting towards a tunnel.

I'd better keep low, or – splat!

He peered down through the hole in the carriage roof, his heart hammering, his hair and clothes whipping in the wind.

Through the hole, Sam could just make out Karita and Amy battling with Illia. Electric sparks flew as weapons clashed. The red-headed woman was dangerous, but Sam's friends were just about managing to keep her contained.

Grom rose to his feet. Spark zoomed around him, but the stone man snatched at her, forcing the little dragon to keep her distance.

As Sam watched, Charlie stirred from where he'd been knocked out and staggered to his feet.

Grom stooped, one huge hand reaching down to grab and crush Sam's cousin.

Charlie's in no condition to fight back yet! I need to get Grom's attention – and quick.

"Hey, ugly!" Sam shouted down at Grom. "Has anyone mentioned that you could stand to lose a bit of weight?"

The stone man stared up at him, the fires seething in his eye-sockets. He let out a roar.

"Come up here and say that!" taunted Sam.

Grom's massive fingers dug into the

melted edges of the broken roof as he pulled himself up.

Sam slithered away down the carriage roof, still anchored by the hook and chain as the train raced towards the tunnel.

I've got to keep him focused on me while Charlie recovers.

"Hey, pebbles-for-brains!" he yelled against the wind. "Mess with me and I'll turn you into a rock garden!"

Grom bellowed in anger as he heaved himself up.

The green fire burned more fiercely in the stone man's eye sockets.

Another few seconds and ...

Sam flattened himself on the roof as the

train plunged into the tunnel.

Cra-ack!

Sam slipped aside as the stone head bowled past him.

Bye bye, granite head! Sam grinned to himself as he lay in the rushing darkness of the tunnel.

When the train burst back into daylight a few moments later, Sam eased himself back down into the carriage. The rest of Grom lay on the floor – a scattering of lifeless stone chunks. Charlie and Amy were fighting Illia, but Karita was slumped against the wall, either winded or hurt.

"Coming!" Sam yelled, swinging down.

Illia eyed them angrily. "This is not over!"

She flung herself towards the broken window and dived out. For a moment, Sam thought she'd be killed by the fall, but then the drone swooped down from nowhere.

Illia snatched hold of the harness and was drawn up into the sky.

Spark landed on Sam's shoulder, hissing angrily.

"Karita – are you hurt?" asked Amy.

"I'm fine," gasped Karita as Charlie helped her to her feet. Varla crawled from under a seat, mewing as she rubbed against Karita's legs.

The train slowed to a halt. An amplified voice sounded on the intercom.

"Due to mechanical difficulties, this train

is leaving service," it said. "A replacement bus should be here in half an hour. I thank you for your patience in this emergency."

Sam looked at the others.

"Mechanical difficulties?" he said. "That's gotta be the understatement of the decade!"

THREE

Charlie leaned into his pedals as he led the others up the steep track to his grandfather's cottage.

Trips to visit Grandad were never this exciting. That's what happens when you add stone monsters to the mix.

They had left the damaged carriage and mingled with the other confused passengers until the replacement bus had arrived.

The bus had dropped them in Brighton an hour later than planned. But all things considered, Charlie thought they'd done pretty well to get there at all.

He paused in the climb, looking back. The town of Brighton stepped down the long hill – a jumble of old and new buildings dropping to wide shingle beaches and the silver-grey sweep of the English Channel. To the left, Charlie could make out the curved marina and the long finger of the Palace Pier, and directly ahead was the slender silver needle of the i360 tower.

Charlie sighed, old emotions rising in him as he gazed at the familiar landscape.

Grandad always said this was the best view in Brighton.

Sam and Amy were riding along behind Charlie, Spark sitting contentedly on Sam's shoulder, purring like a buzz-saw. But Karita was some way down the hill, labouring at her bike, Varla tucked into a shoulder bag.

The other two stopped and turned their heads.

"Are you OK, Karita?" Amy called anxiously.

"I ... will ... be ... fine," Karita panted wearily. "Don't ... worry ... about ... me."

Charlie frowned, remembering how powerful Karita had been before Malvel had sucked the magic out of her Shadow Panther.

She looks fit to drop!

Karita had done well in the fight against that Raven woman, but it had taken a lot out of her.

"We can walk the rest," Charlie said, dismounting.

The track ended at a low stone wall. Brambles straggled around a wooden gate. The garden beyond was a wilderness of weeds and overgrown bushes.

Charlie felt a bit sad as he wheeled his bike up to the front door of the solitary cottage with its empty windows and its moss-covered roof. It was six years since he'd been here, and he hated to see the house looking so neglected.

He stooped and lifted a flowerpot by the doorstep. The key was there, as it always had been. He fitted the key in the lock and opened the door into a musty gloom.

Things inside were just as he remembered. He made his way into the living room and smiled in fond memory – the room was as chaotic as ever, teeming with the contraptions his grandfather loved to invent.

"Wow!" breathed Sam, staring around. "What is all this stuff?"

There were tall cabinets and painted chests and curious mechanical devices

and card tables and animatronic figures, all crammed into the small room – like an antique shop gone mad.

"Grandad loved tinkering with new tricks," Charlie explained. "The whole house is stuffed with his inventions. Once they were perfected, he'd take them down to his show on the pier."

"He did all this on his own?" asked Amy, staring around.

"He had a partner," said Charlie. He frowned. It was an odd name. "Mr Skyrll!" he said, remembering. "We never met him. Grandad was a bit mysterious about him – he said he didn't come from around here."

Sam moved to a metal contraption that

looked like a cross between a typewriter and a fruit machine. "Have you ever thought your tech-whizziness might come from Gustav's side of your family?" he asked, tweaking some levers.

Charlie smiled, loving the idea that he had inherited part of his personality from his Avantian grandfather.

"You break that, you've bought it," he said as Sam poked at the strange device.

Sam pulled his hand away. "You think these things are worth real money?" he asked.

"I don't know," Charlie replied. "But my dad will go spare if anything gets wrecked."

"Copy that," grinned Sam. He looked at

Spark, still perched on his shoulder. "Hear that, girl? No setting fire to anything."

Charlie stopped at the chimneybreast. A swirl of fond memories filled him as he gazed up at a large, colourful poster of a tall, gaunt-faced man with a twirling moustache and a wide, toothy grin.

"That's my grandad," he said, choking just a little.

Grandad was so great – I still miss him like crazy.

There was a top hat on Gustav's head and a black cloak swirled around his shoulders. Circling him to the waist was the sea serpent from the Seeing Eye amulet.

Karita stepped up to the picture. "Gustav

of Colton," she murmured, a catch in her voice. "So much older than when last I saw you – but I remember that smile. Now you are dead, my friend – and I am the last of us." She sighed and turned away.

Charlie had never thought about it before – but he realised Karita and his grandad must have been kids together.

What a strange idea ...

He coughed to clear the lump from his throat. "So," he said briskly. "We should start looking for the Beast egg, I suppose."

"Any idea where your grandad might have hidden it?" asked Amy.

"Not a clue," admitted Charlie. "We'll just have to search room by room."

"Perhaps not," said Karita. "Let us all keep still and silent. Charlie – listen hard and open your mind. If there is an egg here, it may call to you."

They all stood perfectly still.

Concentrate! Come on – focus on the egg. Charlie knitted his brows, hoping for ... *something.*

"Anything?" Sam's voice broke the long silence.

Charlie shook his head. "Not a thing," he said, disappointed in himself.

"Then we'll have to start looking," said Amy. She drew her backpack off her shoulders and placed it gently on the floor. "I brought a torch – just in case."

She slid her hand inside the bag. "Hey, egg, I won't be gone for lo— Ohhh!" She let out a startled cry.

"What is it?" asked Karita.

Amy stared at her.

"My egg!" she cried in a voice that was half alarm and half delight. "It's hatching!"

FOUR

Amy gently lifted the multi-coloured Beast egg from her backpack. She sat down, resting it in her lap.

Coming! said a small voice in her head. *It's going to be fun!*

The others gathered around.

The egg shook, and a crack appeared.

"Prepare to say hello to your Storm Beast," said Karita.

Amy's heart was thundering, and she

could hardly breathe for excitement.

A Storm Beast! What would it look like?

The shell burst open and a lump of damp fur appeared in Amy's lap, about the size of a football.

She stared speechlessly as it lay there, vibrating slightly.

"Oh, wow!" gasped Charlie.

"Awesome," murmured Sam. "But what is it?"

The ball of fur shook itself and the hair sprang out in all directions, doubling its size. It was a mass of different colours – brown and white fur with stripes of yellow and red covered the Beast's small body.

Pointy ears flicked up from a round head.

Monkey-like arms and legs stretched, and a pair of large, deep blue eyes blinked up at Amy from a face with a flat nose and a wide grin.

"Uhhh ... hello ..." Amy said breathlessly.

The Beast's small, wrinkled fingers reached out and touched her hand.

A name popped into her head.

"He's called Wuko," she said, stroking his fine, thick fur.

"How'd you know that?" asked Charlie.

"She just knows," said Karita, smiling. "We always know."

Wuko let out a chattering cry and bounced into action. He swarmed up Amy's arm, leaped from her shoulder and

bounded around the room, as though so full of energy that he couldn't contain himself.

"Wuko, behave!" laughed Amy.

The little Beast launched himself into the air, swiping Sam's baseball cap off his head and landing on the mantelpiece. He put the cap on and sat there gazing cheekily at them, the cap hanging low over his eyes and squashing his ears so they stuck out sideways.

"He's a bit of a handful!" said Sam. Perched on his shoulder, Spark stared at the new Beast with fascinated eyes.

"Does he have any powers?" asked Charlie, cautiously approaching Wuko.

"That is for Amy to learn," said Karita.

Amy got up and walked over to the mantelpiece. "I don't care if he has powers or not," she said. "He's wonderful." She took the cap off Wuko's head and handed it back to Sam. The little Beast blinked at her and its smile widened.

She was about to reach for him when he suddenly sat bolt upright, his ears pricking as though he had heard something. Amy saw his eyes begin to glow with a bright white light that was like electricity.

"Something's happening," she breathed.

Wuko launched himself off the mantelpiece, jumped clean over her head and scampered for the door.

"Follow him," said Karita. "He has sensed something."

Amy and the others raced for the open door. Wuko was already at the head of the stairs. He whisked off to the left. They pelted up the stairs and found him hammering on the closed door to a back room.

Amy turned the handle and Wuko barged through.

The room was full of half finished mechanical devices standing about on tool-benches.

"This was Grandad's tinkering room," Charlie explained.

Wuko dashed across the room and

landed on a wooden chest bound with copper bands. He stared into Amy's eyes, his small leathery hands thumping at the lid of the chest.

"What is it, Wuko?" Amy asked, sidestepping various odd contraptions as she approached the chest.

Chattering, the Beast pointed to copper clasps then jumped on to Amy's shoulder.

Amy released the clasps and the lid sprang open.

They all stared down into a deep black shaft leading down into the floor.

"It's a magician's chest!" Charlie said.

"But why is Wuko so interested?" asked Sam, leaning further. "Hey – there's a ladder. The walls are a bit narrow, but I think we can just about squeeze through."

"Uh ... but should we go down there?" Charlie asked uneasily. "Grandad's creations always had a trick to them."

Before anyone else could speak, Wuko jumped off Amy's shoulder and leaped into the hole, grabbing at the ladder and racing down it head-first.

"Wuko!" Amy shouted. "Be careful!"

"Well, that settles it," Sam said.

"I will remain above with Varla and Spark," Karita said. "I fear I do not have the strength."

Amy was the first to climb into the shaft, her way lit by the bright beam of Charlie's smartphone. Charlie came after her and Sam last.

The drop was about four metres, ending in a small square compartment constructed of riveted metal sheets. Charlie flashed his light around the box. There was a lever on one wall and several openings that looked like the ends of pipes.

"I wonder what this does?" Sam said, eyeing the lever.

"Don't touch it!" warned Charlie.

"OK, *Mom*," murmured Sam. "Anyone see an egg?"

"Nope." Charlie's light hit Wuko, squatting in a corner and holding something that looked like a large pocket watch.

"What have you found?" Amy asked, putting her hand out.

Wuko passed it to her.

It was a golden compass, inlaid with silver designs. Instead of north, south, east and west, there were Guardian sigils; Fire, Storm and Water, as well as the Stealth sigil that denoted Karita's bloodline.

As Amy showed it to the others, the little black needle flickered back and forth.

"Is there an egg?" Karita called down.

"No – but—"

A loud clank interrupted Amy.

"Oops," said Sam from the other side of

the compartment.

"I told you not to touch it!" yelled Charlie, whirling round. Amy saw that the lever on the wall was now facing downwards. "We need to get out of here before—"

Clang!

Far above them, the lid of the chest slammed down.

The metal chamber began to vibrate.

Whoosh!

Fierce jets of water gushed from the open pipes in the wall.

Amy let out a yell as the water struck her, knocking her backwards into Sam and Charlie. She stared down in horror –

the water was already swirling around her ankles.

It wouldn't take long for the chamber to flood.

The chest has locked itself! We're going to drown!

FIVE

Sam battled against a ferocious jet of water that was pounding right into his chest.

One of these days, I might just have to start listening to Charlie.

He grabbed the lever in both hands and strained to pull it up again.

"It's stuck!" he yelled.

"Let me try," said Charlie, activating his Arcane Band. He jammed his axe-head beneath the lever and pulled on the other end. The rusted lever snapped. "Oops."

"We need to get up the ladder!" Amy shouted against the roar of the water.

"You go first, Amy," Charlie told her. He looked at Sam. "Parts of her implants mustn't get wet or they'll stop working. She won't be able to hear a thing."

With Wuko clinging on around her neck, Amy climbed out of the rising water. She began to smash her mace against the hatch.

"You next," Sam ordered Charlie.

"No!"

"How long can you hold your breath? I can swim underwater for two and a half

minutes!" Sam told him. He'd been on his school's swim team back in California.

Charlie blinked at him in amazement then began to climb.

This is so not good! thought Sam. He followed Charlie up, but the water was around his chest now, and rising. "How's it going up there?"

"I'm hitting it as hard as I can!" cried Amy. "It won't budge! Karita is trying to pull it open from the other side."

The water was shooting up the shaft now, bubbling around Sam's neck. He tried to climb higher, but Charlie was in the way.

He took a deep breath a moment before the water rose up over his face.

One hope remained. He'd never tried to communicate with the little dragon over a distance before – but he had to give it a try.

He shut his eyes, focusing on Spark – picturing her in his head – concentrating hard.

Spark? I hope you can hear me – try to melt the locks on the lid.

He felt Charlie's legs kicking, and thought he heard a scream above the noise of the water.

This is it. We're done for.

There was a blur of light above him. A hand reached down into the water, grabbing Sam's collar and yanking him upwards.

Spluttering and coughing, he climbed the last few rungs and was helped out of the deadly chest. His clothes were soaked.

Karita was breathless and pale, a length of wood in her hands where she had been trying to break the lid open.

Spark let out a delighted cry and hovered in front of Sam's face, gently butting foreheads with him. Sam saw that the metal catches holding the lid down had been melted away.

He had never felt closer to the little Beast. "You saved us!" he said. "Good girl!" The dragon purred happily and settled on Sam's shoulder, her tail wrapped around his neck.

"The water's going down again," said

Charlie, peering into the shaft. "I told you Grandad's inventions always had a trick to them."

"Did you find anything down there?" asked Karita.

Amy showed her the compass.

"Intriguing," Karita said. "But I'm afraid we must accept that there is no egg in this house. It must be elsewhere." Her legs suddenly folded under her and Sam and Charlie only just caught her before she fell.

She's used up all her strength trying to open the lid.

They got Karita to a chair. Her face was grey. Varla rubbed against her legs, mewing anxiously.

Amy knelt in front of her. "You have to rest," she said.

Karita nodded. She took her smartphone out. "I'll get a hotel room. I can lie down and sleep for a couple of hours."

Charlie nodded. "While you're resting, we can go to the pier." He looked at the others. "You never know – there might still be some of Grandad's stuff there. He was clearly good at hiding things."

"Let's hope the egg's there," added Amy.

Karita took the compass from Amy and told them she'd message the name of her hotel. "Remember, Guardians, you are strongest together," she said as they cycled away.

"What do you think Wuko can do?" Sam called to Amy as the three friends pedalled along Brighton's bustling seafront. "The little fella is a Storm Beast, after all – maybe he can shoot lightning bolts from his eyes. That would be awesome!"

"Pretty awesome," agreed Amy. Wuko was sitting on the handlebars of her bike. Anyone passing by would have guessed he was a soft-toy mascot.

It was a fine, sunny day and the picturesque seaside town was full of tourists.

"Hey, Charlie," Sam called. "What kind

of Beast do you think you'll get?"

Charlie glanced around at him. "It'll be a Water Beast of some kind," he called back.

"How about a magic talking dolphin?" shouted Amy.

"Yes, that'd be cool," Charlie agreed. "But a giant octopus would be better in a fight."

"It could wear eight boxing gloves," chuckled Sam. "But, knowing Charlie, it'll probably be a cyborg," he added. "Half Beast, half computer."

They all laughed.

"It's like a mini theme park," Sam said, as they walked their bikes along the pier, past food outlets and souvenir stores. Up ahead, he saw a huge white hall filled with computer games.

"Hey, guys," he began, "do we have time to play a few—"

He was interrupted by a yell from Amy. "Wuko – come back here!"

The little Beast zipped past Sam, racing between people's feet, heading for the end of the pier.

Sam parked his bike against the side rail and raced after the little creature. Charlie and Amy were right behind him. They had also ditched their bikes.

"He's sensed something," cried Amy. "I'm sure of it."

"What on earth is that thing?" someone gasped as Wuko nipped between his legs.

"It's a magical Avantian Storm Monkey," Charlie said quickly.

"Very rare!" added Sam.

"But totally harmless!" Amy finished.

They chased Wuko all the way down the pier past a series of rides. There were so many people milling around it was hard to keep sight of him.

"I've lost him!" Sam shouted, skidding to a halt by a Ferris wheel.

"This way!" Amy yelled.

Sam could see that they'd almost reached the end of the pier.

I hope the little guy doesn't dive into the sea!

A large grey shape caught his attention

off the left-hand side of the pier. It was a massive yacht, anchored about five hundred metres out to sea. Something about it made Sam feel uneasy. He saw the name.

Torgor.

He didn't recognise the word, but it gave him a bad feeling.

"In here!" His attention was caught by Amy, who dived in through a small side door in a maintenance building.

With Wuko scampering ahead, Sam and Charlie followed Amy up a flight of wooden stairs. They came into a gloomy, dusty, disused store room.

"Smells kind of funky," said Sam, sniffing.

A cloud of dust rose into the air as Wuko burrowed under a pile of old sacks and blankets.

"He's found something," said Amy. "Help me shift these."

They dragged the filthy coverings aside.

Wuko stood in the middle of a trapdoor. It was held shut with a large padlock in the shape of a sea serpent with its tail in its mouth.

Wuko stared at the children in turn with his big, luminous eyes. Then he tapped his foot impatiently and pointed downwards.

"I think the little guy wants us to go down there," Sam said.

"I think he does," agreed Amy.

"That's funny," Charlie said as he knelt to examine the padlock. "There's no keyhole." But when he touched the lock, the three squiggly waves of the water sigil on his Arcane Band lit up in a golden glow. There was a sharp click as the serpent's curled tail sprang out of the mouth and the lock flipped open on a hidden hinge.

"Awesome!" said Sam with a grin. "What are we waiting for? Let's get down there."

SIX

Charlie heaved the trapdoor open and stared down as a dim blue light ignited below. He could see a metal spiral staircase. A fairground organ began to play a jaunty melody. *Creepy*, thought Charlie.

An amplified, echoing voice rang out.

"Welcome, beloved descendant of the House of Colton."

"That's Grandad!" gasped Charlie, startled and delighted to hear his voice after all those years.

"He's talking to you, Charlie," said Amy. "He must have known you'd find this place."

A hundred questions bounced around inside Charlie's head.

"Descend the stairs, Guardian of Avantia, and seek your inheritance," continued the voice. "Have no fear – wonders await you."

Heart thudding, ears ringing with the eerie music, Charlie climbed down the stairs with his cousins close behind. As he reached the bottom, his grandfather's tinny voice rang out again, playing from some distant speakers.

"Behold the hidden wonders of Professor Colton's Mysterious Voyage!"

Charlie led the others into a circular chamber, lit up in washy blues and greens. The walls flickered like waves. There were animatronic mermaid statues, and the creaking mechanical tentacles of a huge squid flailed from one wall. Clockwork starfish scuttled across the wooden floor

"It's like we're underwater," breathed Sam. "How cool is this?"

Amy gave a yelp as a mechanical shark glided past, hanging from wires. "Not cool! Didn't your parents ever tell you about this place?" she said to Charlie.

He shook his head. "I don't think they knew it existed." He looked at his cousins. "Do you think Grandad hid the egg here?

For me to find?"

"You bet he did," said Sam. "The guy's a genius!"

"You'd have liked him," said Charlie. He walked into the centre of the chamber, trying to take it all in – trying to understand. Beneath his feet, blue and green boards radiated out from a central point, like the spokes of a wheel.

The others followed him, Amy staring around the fantastic room. "Is all of this mechanical and electrical?" she wondered. "Some of it seems … almost – well, magical."

"Maybe," breathed Charlie, his senses hitting overload. *I wish you'd showed me this while you were alive, Grandad.*

"Wuko?" Amy said. "Can you find where the egg is?"

But Wuko just gazed around, his eyes reflecting the greeny-blue light.

"How can we be sure he's even sensing the egg?" asked Sam. "What if he's led us here for nothing?"

"He knows this is the right way," snapped Amy. "I can feel his thoughts. He wants to find it for us."

"Maybe he's like a sniffer dog," said Charlie. "Maybe he can smell the egg?"

"Or can see through walls," said Sam. "His eyes are kind of crazy. Hey!" All around them a row of sharp points rose out of the wooden floor from a long slot circling the room.

Charlie felt a prickle on his neck as his wonder began to be replaced by unease. These mechanisms hadn't been activated in years – what if something went wrong?

There's no way out now.

"Fear not," said his grandfather's voice as if answering his thoughts. "Dangers await. But while your heart remains true, we are certain that nothing will keep you from your destiny."

"'We'?" said Sam.

"Oh – he must mean Mr Skyrll, his partner," said Charlie. "I never met him. They must have worked on all this together." There was a rumble beneath their feet. *That doesn't sound good.*

There was a loud creak from the floor in the centre of the chamber, right where they stood. Charlie watched in horror as a ring of spikes rose around them. *Teeth!* he realised, but too late to do anything about it. A moment later, the boards beneath them separated and the three cousins cried out as they dropped through the floor. *We're falling into a giant mouth!*

They landed with a jolt and began sliding into a long curved tube. Wuko shrieked, scrabbling at the clear plastic sides of the passage. Spark desperately tried to hold Sam up, but there was no space to open her wings. Charlie heard the whir of mechanical parts all around as they fell deeper.

"Oof!" Charlie slid to a stop at the bottom of a wide U-shaped bend. The others slammed into him, punching the air from his lungs. He stood, gasping. There was a purple light around them, mysterious and dim.

"Did I say he was a genius? Your grandad was a crazy man!" panted Sam.

Amy touched her fingers to the sides of her head to check that her coils and processors were still safe in her headband. "We're under the sea," she said, pointing.

Through the clear plastic, Charlie could just make out the sandy seabed beneath him.

There was a sudden lurch as the long

tube turned and began to move rapidly through the water. Bubbles sprayed out from propellers that had sprung from its sides.

"This thing is like a submarine!" said Amy.

"I think we're inside some kind of mechanical sea serpent," said Charlie. "Did you see the teeth? But it can't be anything bad – not if my grandad made it." He looked at his cousins. "Can it?"

"I guess we'll find out soon enough," said Sam.

The mechanical serpent knifed soundlessly through the sea. Soon it began to rise. It came to a sudden stop and the mouth opened into pitch darkness.

"OK, where are we now?" murmured Sam.

Amy shone her phone torch on to a curved roof of rough stone, hanging with stalagmites.

"It's a cave," said Charlie.

They climbed through the mechanical serpent's open jaws and into a large cavern, half filled with water and shelved with stone galleries and walkways that dripped with gleaming seaweed.

The serpent slid away under the water, churning the surface with its propellers. Spark yapped at the giant machine, spitting flickers of yellow flame.

"Great, thanks a lot, serpent dude," said Sam. "How are we going to get back now?"

Amy directed her light around the cave. "Wuko? Can you sense the egg?"

On her shoulder, Wuko growled softly and grasped Amy's hair.

"Apparently not," said Charlie. "Grandad?" he called out. "Why did you bring us here?" His voice echoed back unanswered. As the sound faded, the pool of water behind them began to bubble and ripple.

"Good or bad?" said Sam.

The surface of the pool erupted as a huge squid-like creature burst from the depths. Charlie gasped in horror as it lifted into the air, flying towards them like a rubbery bird, dripping water and clumps of seaweed. Its cruel eyes locked on Charlie and his friends, its long squirming tentacles reaching out.

"Bad!" yelled Amy.

SEVEN

What is this thing? Amy thought, backing off in alarm.

The bulbous creature was a sickly off-white, with huge eyes that glared like lightning. Its enormous, writhing tentacles were lined with suction cups that gave off blue sparks. It swam through the air the way a natural squid would move through water.

Amy watched Charlie and Sam draw

their weapons as the squid dived towards them. Her mace was in her hand almost before she realised it.

She lunged for the creature, giving one of its thick tentacles a double-handed swipe. But the tentacle writhed aside and one wrapped around her wrist. A shock ran up her arm, filling her whole body with pain.

"Don't let it touch you!" she yelled, rubbing her numbed arm. "It's electric!"

"And here I was afraid this was going to be too easy." Sam said as a muscular tentacle whipped out for him. He managed to block it with his shield, but it hit him with enough force to send him crashing back into the cavern's wall.

Amy saw that Charlie was having better luck with his axe. He was able to fend off the squid's attacks, but only just. Its tentacles seemed like they were everywhere at once and never let the cousins anywhere near the bulk of the creature. Spark was in the air, spraying it with fire.

How do we stop this thing?

She tucked and rolled, dodging two of the squid's frenzied limbs, and was able to get close enough to get another look at the creature's strange eyes. They glittered with cold blue-white energy.

The squid caught Amy with the whip of one of his tentacles, and again the pain of electricity thrummed through her as she was knocked back.

"I think it's doing more than just use energy," she shouted to Charlie. "I think it *is* energy. Remember the gargoyle we found in Grandma Fern's cellar?"

"How could I forget?" Sam asked. He'd picked himself up and now stood beside Amy, his hook at the ready. "So what do we do?"

"We use its energy against it," Charlie said. He ducked a tentacle the width of a tree trunk. "Somehow ..." He was out of breath.

I don't know how much longer we can keep this up!

"Come on, Charlie," said Sam. "We need

that big brain of yours. Tell us what to—"
Before he could finish, the squid grabbed
Sam, wrapping him in its tentacle like it
was a boa constrictor and Sam was its meal.

"Sam!" Amy threw herself at the tentacle
that had her cousin, but was snatched up
by another of the squid's limbs in just the
same way.

She struggled against the monster's slimy
flesh but the foul thing was like one giant
steely muscle. Its electricity stung wherever
it touched her skin. It was getting very hard
for her to breathe.

Wuko leaped from her shoulders with a
howl of outrage. He sprang into the whips
of tentacles and vanished.

"Wuko! No!" Amy choked out.

She thrashed against the tentacle that gripped her to try to see where he'd gone.

Finally the tentacles parted enough for Amy to spot Wuko. Her mouth opened in amazement as she watched the little Storm Beast scamper up thick tentacles and dodge the squid's deadly whipping attacks. With a shriek, he leapt for the cave wall. Using his tail to hang from a stalactite, he raised his hands and his feet, then with a furious crackling, the white-blue energy from the colossal squid began to drain, spinning in a whirl into Wuko's four palms. Wuko's eyes gleamed like white stars.

"Of course!" said Amy with glee. "He's a

Storm Beast! He can control energy, like lightning."

One by one, the creature's tentacles went limp and then finally the giant bulk of the creature crashed to the ground. Amy pulled herself loose of the monster's slack flesh.

Wuko let out a wild hoot and began to shake.

"It's too much power for him!" cried Amy in fear.

"I don't think he's done, yet," said Charlie.

Whoosh! In a blinding jet of white light, Wuko sent the built-up energy inside his body smashing into the drained squid. With a boom that shook dust from the cavern walls, the squid exploded into smoke.

Amy's ears were ringing and she adjusted her processors to dampen the sound. Sam and Charlie were staring up at the smoky cloud. Their hair and faces were covered in soot.

"Well, that was cool," said Charlie as he summoned his axe back into his Arcane Band.

With a whoop of delight, Wuko scurried back on to Amy's shoulder. He was breathing heavily, his fur sticking out on end like it was static.

"Wuko, you did it," said Amy, stroking the Beast. He nuzzled against her shoulder.

"He must be connected to energy," said Charlie. "Electricity – magical power – anything like that." He looked at Amy. "There must have been magic in Grandad's secret chamber – that's what led Wuko there."

"He's a handy guy to have around," said Sam. "But what was with the juiced-up squid? Did your grandad put it here?"

"I don't think so," said Charlie. "I think Amy's right. It was like that gargoyle guarding the egg in Fern's cellar. I think the eggs use their magical energy to somehow generate their own guardians to stop the wrong people from getting to them," he went on. "Grandad had nothing to do with it – but he warned us that there would be danger."

"Charlie, you're brilliant," said Amy. "That makes total sense."

"So that means my egg is around here somewhere," said Charlie. "And I'm going to find it!"

He clambered up the rocks, heading deeper into the cave.

"Wait!" called Amy, shining her smartphone light to help him. "We're coming!"

It wasn't easy to keep their footing among the weedy and slippery rocks, but they gradually managed to climb away from the pool and into further watery caves filled with stalagmites and stalactites.

Amy's light shone over a wide stretch of black water.

"What's that in the middle?" asked Sam.

A rocky island rose from the water like a massive stalagmite, its top almost touching the roof of the cavern.

A series of small boulders jutted from the water, forming a steep path to the island.

"Let's find out," Sam said, stepping out on to the rocks.

Amy and Charlie carefully followed Sam up on to the island. Reaching the platform they found, nestled among a collection of shining pebbles, something smooth and curved and blue.

"It's the egg!" Charlie knelt and picked it up in both hands. He stared at Amy and Sam with wide eyes. "I can hear it," he gasped. "It's talking to me!"

EIGHT

My own Beast egg. How great is that?

Charlie held the egg to his ear, but the whispering voice got no louder. There were no actual words – the Beast was just letting him know it was there.

"Is it ready to hatch?" asked Amy.

"I don't know," Charlie replied, thrilled, but a little dazed as well.

A rushing sound filled the chamber and the lake bulged with sudden waves. Charlie felt a strange sensation in his head, like a dull headache. The sense of something coming. Something big.

"What's out there?" said Sam, pointing into the darkness. "Amy – shine your light."

The beam picked out a dark, towering shape cutting through the water. Charlie felt a deep shiver – half fear, half wonder.

"It's your grandad's mechanical sea serpent again," Amy said, with relief.

But when the creature moved into the light Charlie saw a strangely elegant reptile head and a long neck bristling with spines. Its scales were pale green and vivid purple. Its mouth opened to reveal scimitar teeth.

"Bad guess!" yelled Sam, scrambling

away from the water. "It's the real thing!"

In other circumstances, Charlie would have said it was beautiful.

Except that it's terrifying!

The creature let out a roar that shook the cavern and slunk forward. Its head towered eight metres over them, thick coils rising out of the water. Barbs like swords stuck up from its back.

Charlie's first thought was for the egg.

I have to protect it!

As Amy and Sam's weapons grew into their hands, Charlie backed off and carefully tucked the egg into his backpack.

Sam's chain rattled out and the hook glanced off the serpent's neck, the scales

chiming like metal. Spark was in the air, hovering over Sam's head, spitting fire.

Light beams from Amy's torch swung and spun, glinting off the great creature's scales. The serpent ripped up the rocks Charlie was hiding behind with its teeth. With a crunch of its jaws they shattered into dust.

Charlie backed away slowly, climbing the steep slope of the peaked island.

The serpent's head tracked him, eyes shining, jaws open, its long body sliding along the island's rocky shore.

Charlie saw Sam get in a lucky blow, his hook ripping into one of the fins. The serpent's head flicked around, coiling down towards Sam. Spark dived bravely at the monster, but was knocked aside. Amy hit it with her mace, but it was like attacking a cliff-face.

Wuko sprang from her shoulder, reaching for the serpent's towering side. But a whirling fin caught him, and he was sent spinning through the air.

In the low roof of the cave, half hidden by a stalactite, Charlie saw a patch of darkness. It was a slot, like a half open mouth where the uneven roof dipped downwards.

He looked more closely – the lips of rock were the entrance to a slanting hole that seemed to bore its way into the roof.

It's a tunnel! A way out!

"Guys!" Charlie yelled, waving his arms. "Up here! Quick!"

"Coming!" His cousins began to clamber up to Charlie's position. The serpent watched Charlie with its enormous eyes, its tongue licking towards him.

Charlie called on his shield from his Arcane Band and reflected Amy's torch into the creature's eyes. Then he lunged towards the hole in the rock ceiling. *Must be careful of the egg!*

As Charlie reached up for the opening, a shadow fell over him.

He turned, his blood running cold.

The serpent's head was right beside him. He sprawled on the rocks, gaping in horror as the vast mouth opened. He stared past the sharp fangs and down the deep throat. A stench of rotten meat and seaweed made him choke.

The creature's mouth opened around him.

NINE

"**C**harlie-e-e-e-e-e!" Amy's scream of horror echoed around the cavern as the serpent's mouth clamped shut. *He's been swallowed!*

She and Sam scrambled to the ledge near where Charlie had just been. When the serpent reared back, Amy saw Charlie huddled on the rocks, apparently unharmed.

The serpent brought its head down

again, more slowly this time. Its huge eyes stared at Charlie for a few moments, then it turned, slithered down the island and glided smoothly into the depths of the black lake.

Charlie didn't move.

"Hey, Charlie!" Sam yelled. "You're still alive!"

"Am I?" gasped Charlie.

Amy let out a burst of laughter. "Let's get out of here!"

They climbed up the rest of the slope and helped each other into the tunnel opening in the cavern's ceiling.

"Why didn't that thing swallow you up?" Sam asked.

"Maybe it could tell my bloodline is

connected to Water Beasts?" Charlie said. "Or maybe I just smelt wrong."

"Either works for me," Sam said with a grin. Spark chirped from her perch on his shoulder. He turned, peering down the narrow tunnel. "I hope this takes us somewhere safe."

With Wuko clinging to her back, Amy led the way. They crawled in single file up the tunnel. It was a long climb.

She hoped this passage was a straight route to the surface. She knew a lot of caves were warrens of intersecting tunnels and the thought of getting lost here in the dark made her shudder.

"This goes on for ever." Behind her, Sam's

voice sounded odd.

Oh! I changed my processor settings earlier.

Amy switched programmes again.

"... where's the end?" she heard Sam finish.

Just as he said it, Amy saw a dim light ahead. The tunnel ended in an embankment of loose rocks. She began to pull them away, with her cousins helping. When they got through, they found themselves on Brighton beach, the dark sea stretching before them. She was surprised to see that the sky was dark, lit by a full moon. They climbed out of a small hole that had been cut into the concrete of the promenade above the beach.

"What time is it?" Amy asked Sam.

"Just after nine," he replied, consulting her phone. His phone and Charlie's had got wet back at Charlie's grandad's place, and he'd been using hers as a torch while they'd been underground. "Hey – you're almost out of juice."

"Let me see that," Amy said, taking it from him. "The text from Karita with the address of her hotel will be on there."

She read Karita's message. "The Seagull Hotel at 19 Upper Gardens. Room 13." She looked questioningly at Charlie.

He nodded. "I know it. It's not far."

They made their way up through the narrow roads of the Lanes, then past the grand, Indian-style domed building of the Royal Pavilion.

"Here we are," said Charlie finally, as they reached a row of large terraced houses, most of which seemed to be hotels and guesthouses. "The Seagull Hotel."

They opened the front door and trooped up the stairs. At the top of the final flight, a white door with the number 13 on it stood a few centimetres open. Amy felt a twinge of unease.

"Maybe she left it open for us?" said Sam, pushing the door.

They crowded in and came to a sudden halt. Amy gasped.

The bed had been upended and chairs strewn around. The small desk was tipped over and the television was smashed. French windows opened on to a small balcony. Some of the glass panels were broken.

There was no sign of Karita or Varla.

"This is bad," Sam said, stepping over broken glass.

"What's that?" asked Amy, her heart pounding. A small round object stood in the middle of the floor. It had a glistening, greenish surface that moved like dirty oil.

Sam moved forward but stopped as a

beam of green light suddenly projected upwards from the object.

The column of light resolved itself into the shape of a man, bearded and cruel-eyed, wrapped in a dark green cloak.

"Malvel!" Sam snarled.

Amy's stomach tightened in fear and loathing.

"It's a hologram of some kind," breathed Charlie.

"Greetings, children," said the voice of the Dark Wizard. "I have taken Karita and the puny remnants of her Shadow Panther to my ship, the *Torgor*."

"I saw it!" cried Sam. "It's—"

"Shush! Listen!" interrupted Amy.

"Bring your dragon and all the eggs you have collected to the *Torgor*, or Karita and her Beast will suffer." He raised his arms, green flames igniting in his open palms. "Obey me, children. Delay will only cause your friends more harm!"

He flung his arms out and the image exploded in a blaze of cold green fire.

TEN

"**C**areful, Charlie – you'll knock us over!" Sam cried as the small boat tipped wildly in the water. Spark, perching as ever on his shoulder, flapped her wings to keep her balance.

"I told you I couldn't row," Charlie said, struggling with the oar.

"Move in time with me," Sam instructed.

Amy shushed them both. One of her hands pressed her phone to her ear while the other braced her against side of the small boat.

"Hi, Mum. It's Amy. Listen, my phone is down to three per cent, so I'll have to be quick. We're staying with Karita and, er, Tom in Brighton overnight. I'm going to turn my phone off now so there's enough power in it tomorrow to let you know which train we're getting home. Can you tell everyone else that we're OK? Love you."

Amy pressed *send*.

"Do you think our parents will go for that?" Sam asked.

"I hope so," Amy replied. Wuko's eyes gleamed as he stared at the phone from where he lay on Amy's lap. "Hey little guy, don't suck out the last of my battery." He cast a sulky gaze up at her, then let out a sudden shriek.

The small rowing boat glided further from the shore, heading for the eerily lit mega-yacht anchored out beyond the pier.

Once they had recovered from Malvel's blast, the three cousins had wasted no time in getting down to the seafront. Under cover of darkness, they had borrowed a small boat they found tied up in the marina.

Hopefully the owner would get it back before they even knew it was missing.

They had a plan ... of sorts.

But first of all, it meant walking wide-eyed into Malvel's trap.

Across the black water, the Dark Wizard's yacht looked like a big, ugly basking shark, lying out there in deep water, waiting for its prey to float into its open mouth.

Sam eyed the yacht unhappily. *And we're the prey.*

"Is it me, or are the lights getting dimmer?" Amy asked.

She was right. The green-tinged lights that lined the mega-yacht seemed hazier than before.

"It's probably the sea mist," said Charlie. Fog drifted across the little boat, and Sam shivered, although it wasn't cold.

Could this be any creepier?

The bright lights of Brighton faded to a dull blur – even the fairground at the end of the pier was just a wash of cloudy colour.

"At least this helps us get closer without being seen," Amy said.

"Unless Malvel sent it on purpose," murmured Charlie.

"Thanks for putting that idea in my head!" said Sam.

"Karita will be so mad at us for risking our lives to rescue her," Amy said quietly.

"Not when the plan works," Sam said. "Chill out, guys – it'll be a stroll in the park."

I hope that sounded more confident than I feel!

"Careful now," warned Amy. "We're close."

Sam turned, seeing the bow of the huge yacht looming over them in the mist. He pulled in his oar and, when they got close enough, reached for the side of the yacht to pull them alongside it.

Rows of portholes reflected greeny-blue light off the surface of the sea.

"Go, Spark – check it out," Sam whispered.

The little dragon sprang off his shoulder and glided silently along the bows, peering in through every porthole, seeking out any sign of Karita and Varla.

She disappeared into the mist at the prow.

Sam's heart thumped uncomfortably. He didn't like it when Spark was too far away.

"She's been a long time," he whispered

after a few minutes. A feeling of dread seeped through him. "Something's wrong," he murmured.

A shriek sounded from above, cut off short.

"Spark!" Sam bolted to his feet, making the boat rock dangerously.

"What's this?" A familiar, cold voice cut through the mist. "A rat with wings. Stop spitting fire at me, rat, or I'll drown you in a bucket!" There was a flash of white light.

Sam saw Illia Raven lean over the bow, her red hair hanging either side of her pale face, her red lips like a smear of blood. She held Spark by the neck, limp in one gloved hand.

"You're late," she called, throwing down a rope ladder. "Come up and join the party."

With a snarl of rage, Sam activated his Arcane Band. Hook and chain soared up the side of the yacht. The hook caught on the rail and Sam climbed rapidly, all thought of his own safety forgotten as Illia dangled his beloved Beast from her fist.

He vaulted the rail and swung the hook, the speed of his attack almost catching Illia off-guard. She ducked as the hook scythed the air above her head. She fired her stun weapon, but Sam leaped aside as the white blast roared past his shoulder.

"Your Beast is better off unconscious," Illia shouted, flinging Spark to the deck.

"It'll be very painful when Malvel sucks the power out of her."

Sam didn't reply. He had no time for her spite. He swung the hook, driving Illia back so that he could reach Spark.

"Energy lance!" Illia shouted, her scarlet lips spread in an evil grin.

The weapon appeared in her hand.

You don't get near me with that thing!

Sam whirled his hook, eyeing the long thin weapon warily as it sparked and shimmered in Illia's gloved hand. She reared back, her arm rising, ready to throw.

Uh-oh!

The weapon sizzled through the air. Sam jerked his head aside, feeling the heat as it zipped past his cheek.

"Missed!" he shouted.

"Wanna bet?" called Illia. Sam twisted his head in time to see the energy lance turn in a tight bend and come shooting back at him again.

He dropped flat, flicking his chain so it would wind around Illia's legs. But this time she was too quick for him. She leaped high, catching the lance in her hand and flinging it at him again.

Sprawled on the deck, he had no time to get out of the way – but at the last second, Charlie leaped over the rail of the yacht, smacking the lance aside with his axe.

A moment later, Amy jumped on to the

rail, swinging her mace.

"We've got your back, Sam!" she shouted, hurling herself through the air.

Illia fired her stun weapon, but Amy tucked her legs up and the white blast passed beneath her. Illia scrambled away as Amy swung her mace. But Charlie was right behind her, the axe in both hands.

Illia dropped to one knee. "Don't hurt me," she cried. "I'm human!"

Charlie hesitated. Illia swung her legs out, catching him at the knees and sending him flying. She bounded up, laughing.

"Gotcha, sucker!" She aimed the stun gun at Charlie.

Sam whipped his chain, ripping the

weapon from her hand before she could use it.

Amy came up behind her. "Want to try that trick on me?" she asked, her face ferocious.

Illia backed against the wall, her eyes darting from Sam to Amy as they closed in on her. Charlie got to his feet, his axe ready, a fierce light in his usually gentle eyes.

"Where are Karita and Varla?" Amy demanded.

Illia laughed. "That's for me to know and you to guess," she crowed. "The point is, we left that message to lure you here – and here you are, like obedient little puppies."

"Like your worst nightmare, you mean!" Sam snarled.

A harsh voice sounded from the deck above them. "You're the ones who have walked into a nightmare."

Sam snapped his head up. Malvel stood at the rail above, a ring of green fireballs revolving above his head. He flicked his fingers and the fireballs rained down upon the cousins.

One of them exploded in Sam's face. He felt himself tumbling through the air – and then there was nothing.

ELEVEN

Charlie woke up in a world of pain. His head throbbed, and he felt weak and drained. The last thing he remembered was Malvel's green ball exploding in his face.

He and Amy and Sam were clamped to the gunwale of Malvel's mega-yacht by bands of steel that looped around their wrenched-back wrists.

The discomfort drained his spirits –

and knowing how easily they had been captured was crushing. Their attempt to free Karita and Varla had failed miserably.

It was all for nothing!

Malvel stood back, his cloak billowing around him. Illia was shouting in Amy's face. Tucked in the crook of her arm was the blue egg Charlie had found in the cavern. Charlie felt his heart sink.

She must have searched me while I was unconscious.

"Where is the egg you stole from Obsidian Tower?" Illia raved. "Answer me!"

"She can't hear you," gasped Charlie. "She's deaf." He could see Amy's headband and her coils and processors lying on the deck a little way off. *They must have been knocked loose when Malvel's fireball hit her.*

Illia rolled her eyes. "Oh, just what I need!"

"You're some special kind of meathead, lady!" shouted Sam, straining at the metal loops.

Snarling, Illia ran at him, raising her energy lance.

"Calm yourself, Illia," Malvel said smoothly. "Corpses give no information."

Illia hovered over Sam, the lance pointed at his chest. "I could kill this one," she said through gritted teeth, "to get the others to talk."

"All in good time," said Malvel. He took a

step forward. "Listen to me, Guardians of Avantia. You fought well – but the battle is over. The Seeing Eye will lead me to every Beast egg on this planet. It showed me that there was an egg here – hidden by Gustav of Colton." He gestured towards Illia. "We have Gustav's egg, as you see." He frowned. "But I need the egg you took from my laboratory. Tell us where it is, and I will set you free."

"Hold out on us and you'll die," added Illia, her eyes gleaming. "I'm looking forward to it."

I bet you are, you psycho!

Charlie tried to activate his Arcane Band, but nothing happened. Somehow Malvel's bonds had broken the psychic link. They were helpless.

A curious tingling ran down Charlie's spine and flowed into his arms and legs. He turned to look out over the mist-shrouded sea. He didn't know how – but he felt a presence out in the water. Something he'd felt before.

"Kill the girl first," Malvel told Illia. "She's no use if she can't hear us." He strode along the deck to a small silvery bundle lying on the boards. "But first, I shall drain this Beast's power." He stooped and picked Spark up by one limp wing. "She's small, but full of magic."

"No! Leave her alone!" shouted Sam,

struggling in his cuffs.

Smiling, Malvel lifted his other hand, and the emerald gem on his ring began to glow.

Charlie knew what that meant, because he'd seen it happen to Varla. Any second now that ring would suck all the power out of Spark.

But before the ring came to life, all the lights on the yacht faded at once, plunging them into a hazy dimness.

"What's going on?" snarled Illia, pouncing on Charlie and grabbing him by the throat. "Are you brats doing this?"

"You're in for it now!" said Sam.

The yacht's lights flickered then went out completely.

In the sudden gloom, Charlie saw a small furry shape come bounding along the deck with huge eyes that shone like blue-green searchlights. *Wuko! Perfect timing!*

"Get them!" Charlie cried.

All the energy sucked out from the boat lights exploded from Wuko's fingers, knocking Illia to the deck as it passed her, powering towards the Dark Wizard.

Malvel was torn off his feet. Spark fell from his grip as he was hurled backwards down the length of the yacht. Charlie saw his mouth open in a howl of rage as he plunged into the sea.

Spark's eyes opened, and her wings

flapped. She soared upwards, spitting angry flames.

"Set us free, Spark!" cried Sam.

The little dragon swerved in the air and flew along the gunwale behind them, melting the metal loops with careful jets of flame.

Amy sprang forward and scooped up her hearing gear, fitting it in place and looping the band over her head. She touched the processors and grinned. "That's better!" she said. "Wuko! You did great! They didn't know what hit them!"

Keeping Wuko's existence a secret until the perfect moment had been their plan all along – and it had worked exactly how they wanted.

"Wuko?" Amy called again, looking around.

"Where's he gone?" asked Charlie.

"I have him!" snarled Illia. All eyes turned to her. She was squatting on the deck a little way off, pressing down on an inverted plastic crate.

Wuko won't be able to use his energy abilities from in there!

Charlie activated his wristband and the axe flowed into his hand. Hook and chain and mace also appeared as the cousins closed in on Illia.

"One step closer and I'll reach in and throttle the little Beast," Illia threatened. "You won't have time to stop me."

A whirling, gushing sound burst out behind them. Charlie turned to see Malvel – bone dry and smiling – rising out of the sea on a spinning column of water.

The head of the waterspout leaned over and Malvel stepped easily on to the deck of the yacht.

"So, the egg hatched," he said. "Excellent. Now I have two Beasts to feed upon."

All the joy flooded out of Charlie as Malvel strode across the deck.

It's over. We failed.

But suddenly the sensation of an approaching presence again blazed in Charlie's mind. Stronger than before. And angry enough to make him dizzy.

A moment later, the air was split by a ferocious roar as a huge shape burst out of the sea alongside the yacht.

Charlie stared up at an exquisite and graceful reptilian head set upon a long purple and green neck barbed with pointed spines.

His heart stopped, his blood running cold.

The sea serpent from the cave!

The creature stared into Charlie's eyes, and then a friendly hissing rumble came out of its throat, and it licked Charlie's face gently with its long tongue. The giant serpent made the long hissing rumbling sound again. It sounded like *sssskyraaal*.

Charlie laughed in delight as he finally understood. *I know who you are!*

"Two Beasts?" he shouted at Malvel. "Count again!"

The serpent dived, its jaws gaping. Malvel raised his hands, anger and alarm twisting his face, green fire blooming in his palms. But before he could attack, the serpent was on him and he tried to leap aside. He was struck by the Beast's muscular head, which sent him smashing to the deck.

With a flick of his head, the serpent knocked Illia over, bowling her helplessly along the yacht, the blue egg spilling out of her grip.

Charlie hurled himself at the egg and

caught it just before it could roll overboard.

Smiling, he got to his feet, axe in one hand, egg in the other.

"Looks like Grandad hatched a Water Beast of his own. Sam, Amy – meet my grandad's old partner, Mr Skyrll!" He laughed aloud. "Now we've got ourselves an even fight!" he shouted. "Go, Guardians!"

TWELVE

Amy had woken to a world of complete silence, pinned to a railing on Malvel's yacht with Illia screaming mutely in her face.

Her hearing apparatus was part of who she was – how she approached life. To have lost it all was terrifying.

She'd tried to follow what was happening – not to panic – but it wasn't until Spark set her free and she was able to hear again that she felt in control.

Except maybe for the fifty-metre sea serpent!

Wuko! Her first thought was for her Beast. She ran for the crate where he had been imprisoned, vaulting over Illia Raven, who was sprawled on the deck following the sea serpent's attack.

Wuko emerged from beneath the crate, looking outraged.

Amy snatched him up in her arms, breathing in the wonderful scent of his fur.

You're safe! Thank heavens!

Amy quickly took in the situation.

Charlie and Sam were ready with their

weapons and the sea serpent had taken out Malvel and Illia.

I have no idea why it's on our side, but I think Sam and Charlie can survive without me for a little while. I need to go and find Karita and Varla.

Amy dived through a doorway with Wuko close behind.

"Can we have some light, Wuko?" she asked.

The little Beast touched a switch and sizzling energy ran from his fingers into the wall. Dim lights ignited in the ceiling, revealing a narrow corridor.

Wuko had restored some of the drained power of the yacht's electric grid. Enough for Amy to see by, at least.

She ran along walkways and down steep flights of stairs, opening every cabin door and glancing inside before moving on. It was a huge task to search the entire yacht, but Amy was determined not to stop until she found her friends.

She came to a locked door, deep in the bowels of the yacht.

Instantly suspicious, she hammered on it. "Karita?"

A faint voice sounded from beyond.

"Yes. We're here."

Amy's mace slipped into her hand and she gave the door a whack.

It sprang open.

She let out a gasp as she saw Karita, sitting in the room with Varla on her lap.

"You're not hurt," Amy cried in delight.

"No." Karita got up, letting Varla slip to the floor. "I hoped you three had something to do with the lights going out." A hard edge came into her voice. "Is Malvel on board?"

"Yes, a sea serpent knocked him out. It's huge – but it seems to be on our side."

Karita looked questioningly at her. Then she took something from her pocket and the room was suddenly filled with blazing light. It was the compass they'd found at Charlie's grandad's house.

Amy took the device and stared as it lay

on her palm, gushing light. Its needle was a spinning blur.

"I have discovered its purpose," Karita said. "Do you see – three of the sigils are lit up now. Only the fourth – my sigil – is still dark."

Amy leaned into the dazzling light. The sigil of Stealth was the only one from which light wasn't pouring. "Yes! But what does it mean?"

"I think Gustav worked out how to open a portal to Avantia," Karita explained.

"Charlie's grandad really was a total genius, wasn't he?" breathed Amy.

Karita nodded. "That he was," she said. "I could never have accomplished such a feat. This compass can harness the power of Beasts of Water, Storm, Stealth and Fire. Spark is Fire, Wuko is Storm, and the serpent has to be a Beast of Water. That leaves only Stealth."

"But Varla's Stealth power was taken by Malvel," said Amy.

"Yes." Karita's face was grim. "But perhaps something can still be done."

Karita gently lifted Varla into her shoulder bag and they left the cabin, Wuko bounding along the walkways and up the stairs ahead of them.

Bursting on to the deck, Amy was alarmed to see that Malvel and Illia weren't as helpless as she'd hoped. Malvel was floating above the yacht on a disc of green magic light, hurling fireballs at the sea serpent as it snapped at him.

Some of the bolts of green fire were going astray, smashing down through the deck, sending up plumes of swirling poison-green smoke.

Amy could hear creaking and booming from deep in the yacht's hull. Malvel's sorcerous fire was doing serious damage down there.

The serpent had suffered some burns, but it attacked relentlessly and Malvel was struggling to keep it back.

Illia was fighting Sam and Charlie, her energy lance slicing through the air. Spark hovered, snapping at her.

"A Water Beast, indeed!" Karita cried, staring up at the serpent. "How did Gustav hide it all those years?"

At that moment, Illia's lance struck Charlie a glancing blow that knocked him to his knees. She leaped at him and it was only the sweep of Sam's hook and chain that stopped her stabbing Charlie with the deadly weapon.

Wuko stretched out both arms towards Malvel. Twin beams of white light exploded from his palms, but the Dark Wizard seemed to be expecting this, deflecting the bolts of energy with his hands.

He won't be so easy to defeat. And from

the dim glow in Wuko's eyes, Amy could tell that he'd used up nearly all of the energy he'd sucked out of the yacht's electricity system.

Marvel flicked another series of fireballs at the cousins, his emerald ring catching the flare of his attack. Amy dived for safety, but seeing Malvel's ring gave her an idea.

She knelt by Wuko, whispering instructions to him. "But be careful," she said. "And get the amulet from him, if you can. It's around his neck."

They'd need it if they were to find the rest of the hidden Beast eggs.

Grinning and nodding, the little Beast went scurrying up to the yacht's masthead,

leaping easily from radars to receivers, closing in on where Malvel hovered.

Go for it!

Wuko gave a mighty leap and landed on Malvel's back. The Dark Wizard reached around, trying to dislodge him.

Wuko tore the amulet from around the wizard's neck, then jumped into the air. Spinning, he reached out his fingertips and drew beams of purple energy from Malvel's green ring.

Varla's Beast energy!

"No!" the wizard shouted. Wuko spread his arms and legs as he plunged down towards the deck. Amy darted forwards, deftly catching him in her arms.

"Wuko – you're a star!" Amy took the amulet and shoved it into her pocket for safety.

Malvel's magic disc teetered in the air and began to spiral downwards; the wizard fought to keep his balance as it struck the deck.

Wuko bounded out of Amy's arms, fizzing with the magical energy from Malvel's ring. She saw that Karita had taken Varla out of the shoulder bag and put her on the deck.

Wuko touched the little animal's head, releasing the magic energy Malvel had stolen from the Shadow Panther.

The cat vanished in a burst of purple

light that blazed as it grew, sending out shards of deep blue fire.

Amy flung her hand up to shield her eyes. When she looked again, Varla was standing in front of her – restored to her full, magnificent size, her fur like midnight-blue velvet, her eyes shining like the dawning sky.

She opened her jaws and let out a roar that shook the deck under Amy's feet.

"No!" Illia stared at the Stealth Panther, her face drained of blood. "That's not fair!"

"The fourth sigil ignites!" cried Karita. She was holding the compass up, and its light was brighter than ever, bathing the whole yacht in a flare of white.

Karita's power has come back, too!

"Now what?" yelled Sam.

"Now we free this world from the grip of evil!" Karita shouted, turning to aim the compass at the Dark Wizard. "Now we send Malvel back to where he belongs."

Karita pressed the centre of the compass.

A large ring of fire formed on the deck, hissing and spitting as it revolved.

"Awesome," cried Sam, jumping back as sparks rained down all around him.

Amy flung her hands over her face as the fiery wheel flung shards of flame into the night, crackling and snapping like fireworks.

Points of white fire bounced off the

walls and the deck of the yacht. "It's like a Catherine wheel gone crazy!" yelled Charlie.

Malvel staggered back, staring at the portal in horror.

His mouth stretched wide and he let out a desperate scream. "No!"

THIRTEEN

"**Y**es!" Sam yelled, running towards the staggering wizard. "Charlie – with me!"

Green flame sputtered in Malvel's palms as he lurched on the brink of the portal. Beyond the wheel of spinning fire, Sam only saw blackness.

They reached the wizard together, barging him over the threshold of the gaping opening.

Malvel's eyes blazed. "You ... will ... suffer ... for ..." There was a rushing sound like a hurricane wind – and the Dark Wizard was gone.

"Sorry?" Sam called into the void. "I didn't quite catch that."

Amy ran up to them, Wuko cavorting at her side. She turned, showing the amulet to Karita.

"That is a great prize!" Karita said. "Guard it well!"

"Is Malvel gone?" Amy asked her. "For ever?"

Karita walked along the deck with Varla at her hip, her hand in the Stealth Panther's fur. "For ever?" she said thoughtfully. "I cannot promise that – but he will find it hard to return to this world."

"That works for me!" said Sam. He saw a movement from the corner of his eye. Illia Raven was sidling off along the deck. "Hey – where are you going, lady?" he called.

An insincere smile curled her red lips. "Malvel played me," she said, edging away. "I had no idea he was evil – trust me. I'm a good person, once you get to know me."

"You have got to be kidding!" gasped Amy.

Sam saw Illia tap out some kind of command on her wristband. "Hey – cut that out!" he shouted.

"Too late," Illia mocked.

There was a whooshing sound as Illia's drone swooped down from the upper decks. She snatched hold of the dangling harness and it lifted her off her feet.

She soared up into the sky. "See you later," she shouted. "Or not!"

Skyrll reared up, snapping at Illia's legs, but the drone darted aside, whisking her away from the sea Beast's teeth.

"That's annoying!" groaned Charlie. "I hated her more than Malvel. At least he wasn't human."

Loud grinding and groaning noises echoed up through the holes that Malvel's spells had burned through the deck. The yacht rolled a little, so they had to catch their balance.

"I think we're sinking," Amy said. "Malvel's fireballs must have burned right through the hull."

There was a noise of rushing water from below and the whole yacht shook around them.

"I think you're right," said Sam. "We need to get out of here – pronto!"

As Sam spoke, Skyrll's long neck curled down and his massive head turned towards Charlie. Sam was impressed by the way Charlie stood there unflinchingly as the sea Beast's huge eyes stared into his face.

"He's been alone since Gustav died," called Charlie. "He wants to go home." He looked at Karita. "Can he?"

"You can hear his voice?" Karita asked. "Even though you did not hatch him?"

"Not exactly," Charlie said. "But I get what he's thinking."

The portal to Avantia was still open, but it was too small to take Skyrll's bulk.

"He will go home!" Karita said. She moved her hand over the compass. The portal rose from the deck, growing rapidly larger.

Sam stared up at the ring of fire-rimmed blackness as it hung in the air.

Skyrll touched his massive forehead against Charlie's chest.

"Goodbye, Skyrll, have a safe journey,"

Charlie said, stroking the Beast's nose.

"Find more Water Beasts," called Amy as the massive head reared up again. "Start a family!"

Skyrll stared up at the portal for a moment, then hurled himself upwards. His head vanished into the darkness, his great shining body shedding water as it reeled up into the hole in the sky. There was a brief flick of the tail – and then he was gone.

"Awesome!" breathed Sam.

There was a sad, pensive expression on Karita's face.

"You can go, too," Amy said to her. "That's what you've always wanted, isn't it?"

"Now we have the compass, I can open a portal to home at any time," Karita said. "But for now, I will stay on Earth." She smiled around at them. "We have much work to do, Guardians. We have many eggs to find, and this world harbours other dangers than Malvel."

Illia Raven, for one!

Karita touched the compass again and the portal faded away.

"Guys," said Sam as the deck shifted under them. "Sinking boat – remember?"

It was quite a scramble to get over the lurching side of the yacht and safely into the small boat, but they managed it before the tilting of the deck became too dangerous.

Karita took the oars, rowing them quickly away from the *Torgor*, Varla sitting at her feet with shining eyes. Amy and Charlie were in the stern, Wuko nestling in Amy's arms, the blue Beast egg in Charlie's lap.

Sam sat in the prow with Spark on his shoulder. He watched as the yacht wallowed lower in the water. Quite suddenly, it keeled over and slipped beneath the sea.

"It's a shame Skyrll has gone," sighed Charlie. "We were getting on really well."

Sam smiled at him. "You've got your own egg, now."

"One you can hatch yourself," added Amy.

"And the bond between a Guardian and their own Beast is more profound than you can possibly imagine," Karita told Charlie. "As you will learn."

Sam stroked Spark's folded wings. "Yes, it is," he said.

Charlie lifted the egg to his ear. He listened for a few moments then smiled.

"Not yet," he said. "But soon. Very soon."

THE END

Have you read the first New Blood book?

Discover how Amy, Sam and Charlie's story began ...

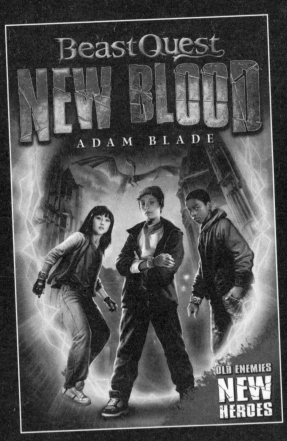

LOOK OUT FOR MORE THRILLING
NEW BLOOD ADVENTURES!

If you enjoyed this book, don't miss
the new series of

BeastQuest

ADAM BLADE

Beast Quest

ELECTRO
THE STORM BIRD

**Read on for a sneak peek at
ELECTRO THE STORM BIRD . . .**

A DAY LONG AWAITED

Tom sat straight-backed on the raised dais near the king and queen, his stomach churning with nerves as he gazed over the crowded courtyard. The jewelled outfits and dress armour of the assembled guests shone in the morning sun, dazzling him. A fresh breeze made the palace flags ripple and snap overhead, and colourful bunting fluttered all along the courtyard walls.

"I'm not used to all this attention," Tom muttered to Elenna, who sat close by his side. Most of the court and palace guard had assembled to watch him receive his powers back. Even his aunt and uncle had come all the way from Errinel. When he caught Aunt Maria's eye, she waved, her face glowing with pride.

"You've earned it," Elenna whispered. "If we hadn't got the Circle of Wizards' artefacts back from the Locksmith, goodness knows what trouble we'd be facing now. Restoring your powers is the least they could do."

Tom had to agree she was right. The Circle's stolen items had accidentally released a fiery Beast called Scalamanx that he'd had to defeat.

"Will the magic lot ever turn up?" grumbled Captain Harkman, from his station just behind them. "It is unforgivable to keep the king and queen waiting like this."

A sudden flash of white light blinded Tom, and startled yelps and gasps ran through the crowd. When Tom's vision cleared, he saw two figures in flowing purple gowns edged with gold, standing on the dais before Hugo and Aroha – Sorella, the head of the Circle, and a young wizard, Stefan. Beside them, two burly men in armour carried a hefty-looking chest. The king and queen smiled welcomingly, but Sorella and Stefan turned away to face the crowd without giving them so much as a nod.

Read ELECTRO THE STORM BIRD
to find out what happens...